Visit us on the Web at www.clavis-publishing.com.

Masato's Garden written by Jerry Ruff and illustrated by Maya Onodera

ISBN 978-1-60537-711-7

This book was printed in May 2022 at Nikara, M. R. Štefánika 858/25, 963 01 Krupina, Slovakia.

First Edition
10 9 8 7 6 5 4 3 2 1

Written by Jerry Ruff
Illustrated by Maya Onodera

Masato's
Garden

Clavis
NEW YORK

Johnny and Masato were playing in the sandbox.
Johnny had made a circle of small stones.
Inside the circle were his toy cannon and soldiers.
Masato ran his finger through the sand.
"What's that?" asked Johnny.
"A river."
"Where's the water?"
"It's in my head," said Masato.
"My grandpa is sick," said Johnny, adding a stone to his circle.
"That's too bad," said Masato. "I'm sorry he's sick."

Johnny picked up a stone. This stone was bigger.
He threw the stone as hard as he could at a nearby
tree. *Thuck!*
"No throwing rocks!" Johnny's mother called from
the park bench. She was sitting with
Masato's mom and talking.

Johnny picked up another rock. It felt smooth in his hand.
He looked at his mother. He put the rock down.
"I don't like my grandpa being sick," said Johnny.
"Me either," said Masato.

The boys played.
Johnny shot the cannon,
then tipped over dead soldiers.

Masato said there were golden fish
swimming in his river. "Koi fish," he
said. "For your grandpa to be strong
and get better."

After a while, Masato said, "Let's go to my house."

Masato lived in a small white house not far from the park.
Johnny had never been there before, and his stomach felt tight.
"You want to see our garden?" Masato asked.
"Lead on, captain," said Johnny.

Masato led Johnny to a large sliding door by the kitchen. He slid the door open, and the boys stepped outside onto a wooden walkway.

"That's not a garden," said Johnny.
He thought of his grandfather's garden.
Sometimes Johnny helped pull weeds
or pick beans and tomatoes.
This was different.
"It's like a sandbox, but with rocks."
"It's a rock garden," said Masato.

Indeed, Masato's garden was filled with tiny pebbles. A few small trees grew at the edges. In the middle sat three large rocks with a patch of tall grass.

Rocks for climbing and grass for hiding, thought Johnny.

"Let's play fighting guys," he said.

"It's not for playing," said Masato.

Johnny felt the toy soldiers and cannon in his pocket.

He wanted to say, "Why not?" but then he felt how quiet everything was. "What's it for?"

"Meditating," said Masato. "My dad sits out here before work. Sometimes I sit with him. It helps him not worry so much."

"What does your dad worry about?"

"Sick people. He's a doctor."

"So where do you sit?"
asked Johnny.
Masato pointed to several
pillows at the end
of the walkway.
The boys sat down
together on the pillows.

"The pebbles are the ocean," explained Masato. "My ojiisan
rakes them and makes swirls like waves in the ocean."
"What's your ojiisan?"
"My grandpa. He lives with us."

"I like the big rocks in the middle," said Johnny.
"Those are mountains. And islands. One's a turtle,"
said Masato.
Johnny looked again at the rocks. He thought about
Masato's river in the sandbox and the golden fish.

After a while, Johnny asked, "Do your dad's sick people get better?"
"Sometimes. Not always. My dad told me he can't make everyone better."
Johnny thought about his grandfather. He might not get better, either.
The boys sat at the edge of the garden. Everything was quiet.

Now Johnny heard a water sound. He looked.
A hollow stick was trickling water into a rock bowl.
Johnny closed his eyes.

Trickle-trickle-trickle
went the water.

Shish-shish-shish
went the tall grass.

Now Johnny could see his grandfather swimming—swimming easily alongside the old sea turtle. The swirls in the pebbles made gentle waves.

In a shady corner of the garden, a plum tree bloomed
pink with blossoms. The trunk of the tree was gnarled.
Johnny thought of his grandfather's hands, planting
seeds in the black dirt, dirt in his knuckles, his fingers
thick and bent, but still strong.

"How old is your grandpa?" Johnny asked Masato.
"My ojiisan? Pretty old."

Johnny looked at the garden, at the rock that was a turtle. He felt a little better, a little less worried now.

"My grandpa's pretty old too. We should go look at his garden. You can pick some beans if you want to."

"Sure," said Masato. "I'd like that."